KV-194-801

 St John Fisher Catholic School

Pinner

HA5 5RA

Written by Renée Edwards
Illustrated by Bob Gauld-Galliers
Designed by Tam Ying Wah
Story Consultant and Magic Wanda poem written by Barbara Chinn
Cover Photography by Dale Curtis
Edited by Jacqueline Fortey and Evelyn Hunter
Activity Designed by Wendy Swan

First edition published April 2005
Printed and bound by Thomson Press
www.MagicWandaMedia.com
ISBN 0-9548715-0-2

MAGIC WANDA

Cloaked by fluffy white clouds up in the sky,
The Island of Nimbi slowly floats by.
It's home to Wanda, Baz and Nubinu,
Richie, Mix-it-well, Mo and Doowott too!

Whilst moonbeams play and you're sleeping at night,
Mix-it-well rides on his Stirring-wheel bike.
He pedals away making magic steam,
Which drifts down to earth to bring you your dreams.

When morning comes to chase the night away,
You wake up and get ready for your day.
If you forget everything you've dreamed about,
From Volcano Mo your dream stuff pops out!

PLOP! Onto the Dream Dump your dreams then fall,
And Doowott turns up to tidy them all!
He never knows what magic he will find,
Lost and forgotten by your sleepy mind.

Wanda
the Dragon

Doowott
the Dragonflyer

Baz Nubinu Spotted
Richie

Dream Dump

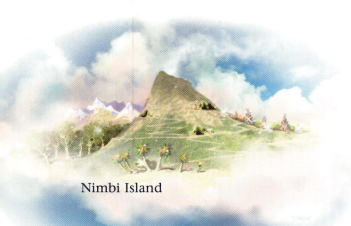

Nimbi Island

Volcano Mo

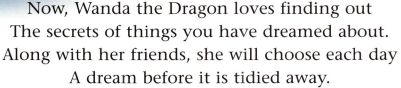

Now, Wanda the Dragon loves finding out
The secrets of things you have dreamed about.
Along with her friends, she will choose each day
A dream before it is tidied away.

The dragons then take the object they've found,
And fly through the Dream Steam, down to the ground.
They find the dreamer and give back the dream,
To discover what this special dream means.

Once they have found out all there is to know,
Through the Rainbow Gate to Nimbi they go.
They share with Mix-it-well what they have learned
About the special object they've returned.

Who knows, one day perhaps Wanda will bring
a dream back to yoooooooooou!

Everard
Mix-it-well

_____

I am the owner of this book

Dream-finder

For Louis, Raphael and James

MAGIC WANDA
AND THE SCULPTOR

written by

Renée Edwards

illustrated by

Bob Gauld-Galliers

Magic Wanda Media, London

One morning, Wanda the Dragon was sleep-flying lazily above the Dream Dump. She was dreaming about making something special.

"What can I make?" she thought.

In People Land, below, Joe the Sculptor
dreamt about making a cow, a beautiful cow.
Yet, when the alarm went off, Joe forgot
his dream and thought about his
breakfast instead.

Back up on Nimbi Island, inside Mo the Volcano, Everard Mix-it-well pedalled his Stirring-wheel bike, creating the steam that makes us dream.

Mo the Volcano spat out the last of the night's forgotten dreams. Out popped Joe's cow.

SPLOSH!

Doowott felt cross.

"Tut, tut, tut! What a big ugly thing," muttered Doowott.

"How am I going to tidy it away?"

Wanda's friends were looking for Wanda.

"There she is, sleep-flying again," said Nubinu.

Then the dragons noticed a big animal making its way slowly towards Wanda.

"Oh my!" said Nubinu. "Is it a giant slug?"

"What's it going to do?" asked Richie.

"Let's see if it wants to play!" said Baz.

"What, now?" asked Richie, adding loudly, "Wanda, wake up! I think there's a monster!"

"Wakey-wakey, sleepyhead!" said Nubinu.

Wanda began to stir and noticed the giant animal with her sleepy eyes. Wanda quickly landed on the ground.

"What's this?" she exclaimed.

Then she heard a little grumpy voice.

"I don't know," answered Wanda,
"but it wants our help."

Wanda leant forward and asked slowly,
in a loud voice:

What is the matter?
How can we help you?

The grumpy voice continued,

"I'm very busy. I've got lots to do! Let me
out of here you dizzy dragons!" it said.

"Well," said Nubinu, "it's very rude, whatever it is!"

"Yes!" added Baz. "Reminds me of..."

Suddenly Doowott buzzed out from underneath the cow.

The dragons jumped back in surprise.

"DOOWOTT!"

"Did it eat you?"
asked Richie, flabbergasted.

Everard Mix-it-well was on his morning walk,
"Good morning all, what have we here?
  A mysterious object, that is clear."

"It's only pretend," said Wanda.
"We thought it was real!"

"This special object of someone's dream
    Is fascinating in the extreme!"
said Mix-it-well.

"Would you like to take it and learn
    Its secrets to share on your return?"

The old dragon placed the magic
    Dream-finder around Wanda's neck.

"This will help you find your way.
    Please come home by playtime today."

So the four young dragons flew off
with the animal.

At last Doowott smiled.
"Good, now I can get on with my work."

The Dream-finder led the young dragons
through the Dream Steam to People Land.

The dragons landed in a field of cows.
They had never seen real cows before.

"Looks like we've found the right place," said Nubinu.

"There are lots of them, and they're coming our way," reported Baz.

"I don't like this," said Richie.
"They are like this one, but real."

When the cows came up to the dragons and started to lick their faces, Richie began to laugh.

"Yuk!" said Nubinu.

One of the
cows licked the
Dream-finder from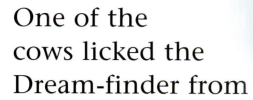
Wanda's neck and it flew into the air.

Nobody saw where it landed.

"Oh! Oh!" said Richie.

"This is silly!" said Baz. "I know, let's
hide under here and run like mad."

"We'll find the Dream-finder later,"
said Wanda.

It was dark inside the cow, so the dragons couldn't see where they were going and they crashed into a wall. The cow broke into pieces. The wall was part of Joe the Sculptor's workshop.

"We're dragons from Nimbi, the island of
   dreams," Wanda answered. "We're very
   sorry because we've broken your dream cow."

"I did dream about making a cow
   sculpture last night," said Joe.

"What is sculpture?" asked Wanda.

"I'll show you," said Joe.

Joe led the dragons into his sculpture
workshop. It was full of interesting objects.
They were sculptures he had made all by himself.

"This is what I do," said Joe.

"It's my job and my passion. I'm an artist.
I like to make models for people to enjoy."

"Wow! A cow made of wood," said Wanda.

"Yes," said Joe, "I'm making a cow.
  I'm opening a sculpture park for the
  children in the village."

Joe opened two big barn doors to
reveal a field full of animal sculpture.

"I copied these from real animals on
the farm," he said.

"Ooh," said the dragons,
"they look very real!"

Richie put his hand out
to touch a duck.

"Oh!" laughed Joe,
"That IS a real duck!"

"Sometimes I make abstract sculpture too," Joe said, "sculpture to remind me of something. I made this one with shells when I was a little boy, to remind me of the seaside. You can use anything to make sculpture."

"Shall we finish making the cow together?" asked Joe the Sculptor.

Together they finished the cow by covering
the wooden frame with mashed-up paper
in water.

"This is called papier-mâché," said Joe.

Then they painted the cow. When the paint
was dry they carried it outside, and the
children came to play in the sculpture park.

Everyone had a wonderful afternoon
playing on the animal sculpture.

The children were very happy because
Wanda and her friends were there too.

When the parents came to take their children home, Wanda realised it was time for the dragons to go home too.

"Come and see us again," said Joe.

"I love sculpture," said Richie.

The dragons went through the workshop and into the field.

"Look!" laughed Baz, pointing to a cow.

One of the cows was eating some hay, and she didn't realise she was chewing the Dream-finder. It must have landed in the haystack.

"May we have our Dream-finder back, please?" said Wanda.

The cow opened her mouth and said, "Moo!" and gave the slobbery Dream-finder to Nubinu.

"Thank you," said Nubinu and grimaced at her slobbery hand. All the cows mooed.

The dragons flew off to Nimbi Island.
They swept through the Rainbow Gate
to the Dream Dump.

They showed their new skills
to Mix-it-well and Doowott
by making a giant shining sun.

When it was finished they hung it up high.

"It's amazing what we can learn
   From the dreams we return,"
   said Everard Mix-it-well.

"Thank you all for letting us see
   How much fun making sculpture can be."

"We're very lucky! I think we live in
   a giant abstract sculpture park,"
   said Wanda in delight, chuckling.

Suddenly, as if to signal the arrival of Dream-time, which for the dragons is bedtime, Mo the Volcano began humming a lullaby, and spat out the first dream of the night. PLOP!

A big drum landed nearby and rolled up to them.

"Wow!" said the dragons, "What's this?"

"Why, oh why, do people have such big dreams?" said Doowott.

HOW TO MAKE A
GIANT SHINING SUN

What do I need?

- Paper plate
- Stiff paper or card
- 2 empty holders from a cardboard egg box
- Red or orange tissue or crêpe paper
- Paint and brushes
- Glue
- Optional – googly eyes, glitter and any other decorative stuff you'd like to use.

How do I make it?

1. Turn the paper plate over, paint the back yellow and set it aside to dry.

2. Using the stiff paper or card make lots of hand prints with red and yellow paint. Discover what happens when red and yellow paint are mixed and then make some orange hand prints too!

3. If you've got some glitter you could shake it on the wet hand prints before they dry.

4. Next, paint the egg boxes to make some eyes – they can be any colour you like! Or you could paint them yellow and stick some googly eyes on the top instead.

5. Ask an adult to help you cut or tear a strip from the tissue or crêpe paper. Twist the paper strip into a sausage shape, and bend it into a curve. Then use glue to stick this smiley mouth on to the plate.

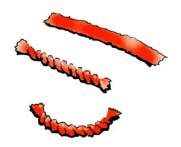

6. Use glue to stick the egg box eyes on to the plate.

7. Add any other decoration you like to make the sun shine!

8. Cut out each hand print and stick them around the rim of the plate to form the rays.

FOR ADULT HELPERS

What will children learn?

As well as stimulating an interest in 3D shapes, making this 'shining sun' will help children to develop skills in cutting, twisting, sticking, printing, and painting. It can also be used as a starting point for talking about colour and texture. It can be exciting for a child to discover the magic of mixing colours together!

More fun ideas

To make the project a little more complex, 3D features (eyes, eyebrows, cheekbones, etc.) can be modelled out of screwed up newspaper and taped into place on the paper plate. The plate can then be covered with strips of kitchen roll dipped in a mixture of half water and half white glue (water soluble). Press the strips around the facial features. Once it's dry the papier-mâché can be painted and decorated as before.

Book credits

Copyright © 2005 by Magic Wanda Media
(a division of Gobsmack Productions Limited)
Published by Magic Wanda Media (a division of Gobsmack Productions Limited)

Written by Renée Edwards
Illustrated by Bob Gauld-Galliers
Designed by Tam Ying Wah
Story Consultant and Magic Wanda poem written by Barbara Chinn
Cover Photography by Dale Curtis
Edited by Jacqueline Fortey and Evelyn Hunter
Activity Designed by Wendy Swan

Acknowledgements:
Renée thanks everyone who has contributed to this book and DVD; a big thank you to Barbara Chinn, Bob Gauld-Galliers and Kim Lombard for their constant support and good humour.

Special thanks to Aim Image, The Barbara Hepworth Museum, Ishara Bhasi, Hilary Baverstock, Gill Baxter, Gavin Bell, Tim Bryant, Cemil Giray Alyanak, Henry Cobbold, Cheryl Cohen, Nic Crampton, Katie Chebatoris, Richard Dove, The Edit Store, The Edwards-Taylor family and friends, Catherine Gang, Debbie Gray, David Harrison, Nick Hedge, Kall Kwik Ealing, Lemur the dog, Jag Matharu, Sarah McCartney, Mary Reynolds, Toby Rushton, Mr and Mrs Sale, Jonathan Sale, Rachel Salter, Tim Waterfield, Jane Wilford, Natasha Wray and the People of ST IVES.

First edition published April 2005
Printed and bound by Thomson Press
www.MagicWandaMedia.com
ISBN 0-9548715-0-2

DVD credits

Presented by Magic Wanda Media
Written, Produced and Directed by Renée Edwards
Narrated by Fenella Fielding
Sand Sculpture by Andrew Baynes
Starring the McLean Family

Director of Photography: David Langan
Sound Recording by Nick Reeks
Second Camera by Robert Wilkins

Animation by The Icing
Music Production by Andrew Belling and Kim Lombard

Audio Post Production by Andrew Sears and Jeff Richardson
Online Editing by Michael Sanders

Production Manager: Cheryl Hernandez
Voice Casting by Mandy Steele
Costumes by Sophie Smith
Photography by Dale Curtis

Rostrum by 2p Films
DVD Authored by The Pavement
DVD Face by Tam Ying Wah
Web Design by Instinct Media

Website: www.MagicWandaMedia.com

Magic Wanda and the Sculptor
Listen to Fenella Fielding narrate the story (11 mins)

Louis and the Sand Sculptor
Watch Louis discover sculpting (9 mins)

Making Sand Sculptures
Learn sand sculpting with Andrew Baynes (4 mins)

Magic Wanda Karaoke
Wanda Sing-a-long (1 min 25 secs)